D0842827

The Little Fish
in a Big Pond

illustrated by Teresa O'Brien

Published by Child's Play (International) Limited

© M. Twinn 1989   ISBN 0-85953-391-3 (soft cover)   Printed in Singapore
ISBN 0-85953-390-5 (hard cover)

Once, in a big pond, a tiny fish hatched from an egg. He and his many brothers and sisters scurried about together.

Life in the pond was hard.
Frogs gobbled up the best food.

From nowhere, terrifying creatures appeared
and snatched up the tiny fish's companions.
But he learned to keep out of harm's way.

"I am a very smart fish," he decided.
"I am a fish with brains."

The little fish was often frightened
by larger fish racing up and down.
Sometimes, he listened to them bragging:
"I swam up the creek as far as the bridge in one minute!"
"That's nothing! I have been to the end of the world,
where the water falls over the edge!"

Time passed. The tiny fish grew into a little fish.
He began to wonder more and more
about the world beyond the pond.

"I am not only a fish
with brains," he thought.
"I have imagination, too.
It is time to make plans!"

In the Spring, the melting snows swelled
the mountain stream. The pond overflowed.
The little fish boldly took his chance.

The raging torrent
swept him down the creek.

The water rushed under the rickety wooden bridge and on to the roaring waterfall.

"The edge of the world!" the little fish gasped. "I'll never see my pond again!"

Dizzily, the little fish tumbled over the waterfall and into the frothing water below.
For the first time he glimpsed the clouds and the sky high above.

Beyond the waterfall,
the stream ran wild and fast.

As he rode the roller coaster rapids,
the little fish felt
that his gills would burst.

The stream joined the wide river, flowing
on and on until it poured into a great lake.

"At last, a home fit for me!" gasped the little fish.
"My pond was not so big after all!"

The little fish learned many things in the great lake.
During Spring, food was easy to find. As he grew stronger,
he learned to jump through the skin at the top of the water
to catch small insects.

At night he would jump
just to see the stars and the moon.
He wondered if he might be able to visit them one day.

But the lake was not free of danger. There were fish and strange monsters of awesome size. Whenever the little fish thought he had seen the largest creature in the universe, another would appear that was twice as big.

So, the little fish searched high and low
for a hiding place, until, at the bottom
of the lake, he found a tin can.

And there he hid, whenever danger threatened.

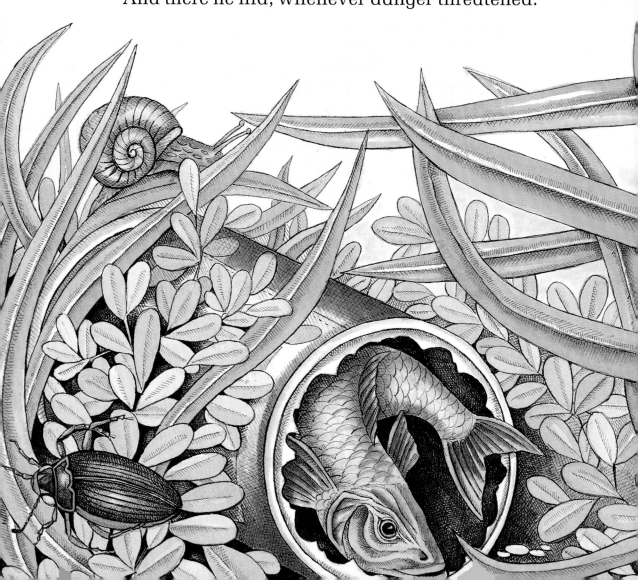

Sometimes, food was scarce in the lake. At other times,
the water turned an evil yellow colour and stank.
On hot Summer evenings, it was almost impossible to breathe.

The little fish hardly ever saw any fish as small as himself.
Those that he met would not talk and did not stay. He was
so lonely, he would have welcomed the company of a frog.

"I wish my pond was not so far away!" he sighed.
'What use are brains,
imagination and plans,
if you don't have a friend?"

But he knew he would never
be able to return and
he pressed himself as snugly
as he could into his tin can.

"I'll never leave my tin can.
No matter what!"
the little fish sighed.

The little fish might have stayed forever,
if it hadn't been for the shiny hook:
the shiny hook that struck the tin can
and lifted it out of the water.

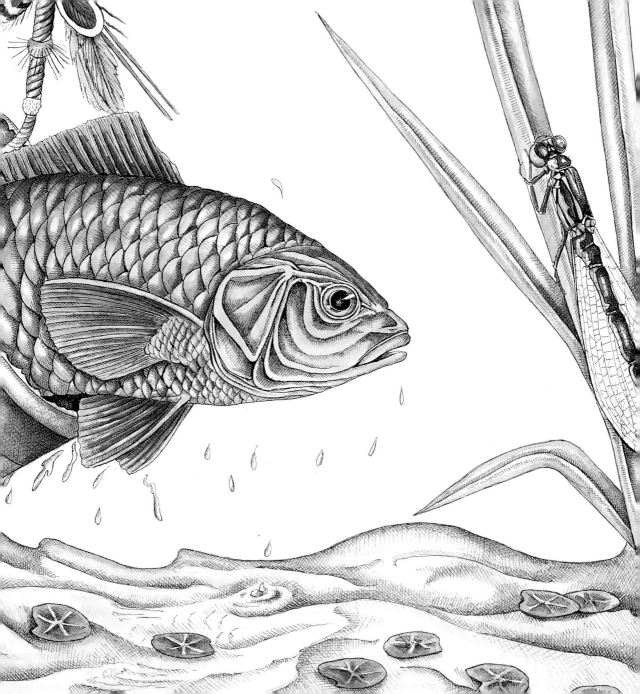

"Look!" a boy cried. "It's a miracle.
I caught a fish in a can!"

"We'll take him home and cook him for dinner,"
his mother said. "Leave him in the can.
Your Dad will never believe it."

The boy placed the tin can in the back
of their pick-up truck, and they drove off
down a dusty road.

The little fish stuck out his head and watched
as the truck drove away from the great lake. It followed
the wide river and the swift stream. It sped past
the roller-coaster rapids and the roaring waterfall.
As the tin can rocked, the water splashed out, drop by
drop.

"This is the end!" the little fish sighed.
"I am going to die!"

Just then the truck began to cross a rickety wooden bridge.

"It's my pond!" the little fish cried.
"My dear pond I left behind so long ago!"

His heart swelled and he felt a yearning deeper than
the great lake. With a splash of his tail, the little fish
jumped out of the tin can . . .

. . . over the bridge

. . . and into the pond.

"I must find another tin can," the little fish thought, diving to the bottom. But as he looked around, everything had changed.

"My pond has grown smaller," he thought. "And all the creatures have grown smaller, too. I don't need a tin can to hide in any more! This pond is a good place to live!"

"It is just the right size for me!"

The pond creatures listened open-mouthed to the fish's
stories about the waterfall, the stream, the rapids, the
great lake, and the universe. They trembled when he told
them about monsters, men with nets and boys with hooks.
From now on, the creatures shared the pond equally.
The larger fish were careful and the frogs were polite.

The wise fish was their chief

''Set your sights high, but don't get out of your depth
Give your imagination room, but be satisfied
with who you are and what you have. Like me. A big fish
in a small pond. Now what are you all gaping at?''

Then the old fish would curl up in a bathtub
which someone had thoughtfully thrown
into the pond and dream about the sky
and the stars and the moon